HELLO, I'm THEA!

I'm *Geronimo Stilton*'s sister. As I'm sure you know from my brother's bestselling novels, I'm a special correspondent for *The Rodent's Gazette*, Mouse Island's most famous newspaper. Unlike my 'fraidy mouse brother, I absolutely adore traveling, having adventures, and meeting rodents from all around the world!

The adventure I want to tell you about begins at Mouseford Academy, the school I went to when I was a young mouseling. I had such a great experience there as a student that I came back to teach a journalism class.

When I returned as a grown mouse, I met five really special students: Colette, Nicky, Pamela, Paulina, and Violet. You could hardly imagine five more different mouselings, but they became great friends right away. And they liked me so much that they decided to name their group after me: the Thea Sisters! I was so touched by that, I decided to write about their adventures. So turn the page to read a fabumouse adventure about the

THEA SISTERS!

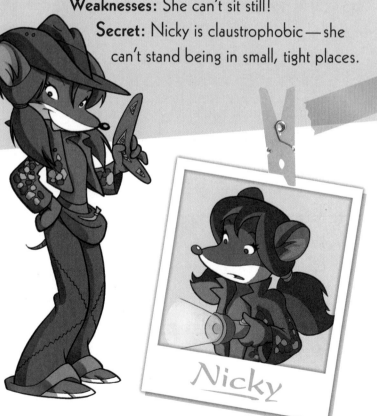

Name: Nicky

Nickname: Nic

Home: Australia

Secret ambition: Wants to be an ecologist.

Loves: Open spaces and nature.

Strengths: She is always in a good mood, as long as she's outdoors!

Weaknesses: She can't sit still!

Secret: Nicky is claustrophobic — she can't stand being in small, tight places.

Nicky

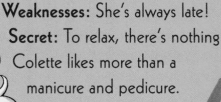
COLETTE

Name: Colette

Nickname: It's Colette, please. (She can't stand nicknames.)

Home: France

Secret ambition: Colette is very particular about her appearance. She wants to be a fashion writer.

Loves: The color pink.

Strengths: She's energetic and full of great ideas.

Weaknesses: She's always late!

Secret: To relax, there's nothing Colette likes more than a manicure and pedicure.

Colette

VIOLET

Name: Violet

Nickname: Vi

Home: China

Secret ambition: Wants to become a great violinist.

Loves: Books! She is a real intellectual, just like my brother, Geronimo.

Strengths: She's detail-oriented and always open to new things.

Weaknesses: She is a bit sensitive and can't stand being teased. And if she doesn't get enough sleep, she can be a real grouch!

Secret: She likes to unwind by listening to classical music and drinking green tea.

Violet

PAULINA

Name: Paulina
Nickname: Polly
Home: Peru
Secret ambition: Wants to be a scientist.
Loves: Traveling and meeting people from all over the world. She is also very close to her sister, Maria.
Strengths: Loves helping other rodents.
Weaknesses: She's shy and can be a bit clumsy.
Secret: She is a computer genius!

PAULINA

Name: Pamela
Nickname: Pam
Home: Tanzania

PAMELA

Secret ambition: Wants to become a sports journalist or a car mechanic.

Loves: Pizza, pizza, and more pizza! She'd eat pizza for breakfast if she could.

Strengths: She is a peacemaker. She can't stand arguments.

Weaknesses: She is very impulsive.

Secret: Give her a screwdriver and any mechanical problem will be solved!

Pamela

Geronimo Stilton

Thea Stilton
AND THE
ICE TREASURE

Scholastic Inc.

New York   Toronto   London   Auckland
Sydney   Mexico City   New Delhi   Hong Kong

No part of this book may be reproduced, stored in a retrieval system, or transmitted in any form or by any means, electronic, mechanical, photocopying, recording, or otherwise, without written permission from the copyright holder. For information regarding permission, please contact: Atlantyca S.p.A., Via Leopardi 8, 20123 Milan, Italy; e-mail foreignrights@atlantyca.it, www.atlantyca.com.

ISBN 978-0-545-33134-0

Copyright © 2008 by Edizioni Piemme S.p.A., Via Tiziano 32, 20145 Milan, Italy.

International Rights © Atlantyca S.p.A.
English translation © 2011 by Atlantyca S.p.A.

GERONIMO STILTON and THEA STILTON names, characters, and related indicia are copyright, trademark, and exclusive license of Atlantyca S.p.A. All rights reserved. The moral right of the author has been asserted.

Based on an original idea by Elisabetta Dami.
www.geronimostilton.com

Published by Scholastic Inc., 557 Broadway, New York, NY 10012. SCHOLASTIC and associated logos are trademarks and/or registered trademarks of Scholastic Inc.

Stilton is the name of a famous English cheese. It is a registered trademark of the Stilton Cheese Makers' Association. For more information, go to www.stiltoncheese.com.

Text by Thea Stilton
Original title *Il tesoro di ghiaccio*
Cover by Arianna Rea, Alessandro Battan, and Ketty Formaggio
Illustrations by Alessandro Battan, Jacopo Brandi, Flavio Ceccarelli, Francesca Colombo, Paolo Ferrante, Michela Frare, Sonia Matrone, Arianna Rea, Maurizio Roggerone, and Roberta Tedeschi
Color by Tania Boccalini, Concetta Daidone, Ketty Formaggio, Edwin Nori, Elena Sanjust, and Micaela Tangorra
Graphics by Paola Cantoni with the help of Michela Battaglin

Special thanks to Beth Dunfey
Translated by Emily Clement
Interior design by Kay Petronio

12 11 10 9 8 7 6 5 4 3 2   11 12 13 14 15 16/0

Printed in the U.S.A.   40
First printing, December 2011

RAiN, RAiN, GO AWAY!

It was a miserable evening in New Mouse City. I was headed home after a whole day in the office, and every inch of my fur was soaking wet.

As you know, dear reader, I work at *The Rodent's Gazette*, the most famouse **newspaper** on Mouse Island. My brother, Geronimo, is the publisher, and I, THEA STiLToN, am a special correspondent.

Now, I'm not usually a desk editor. To me, spending a whole day shut up in the office is a real pain in the tail. But Geronimo had asked me to cover for him, since he was taking the

1

day off to spend time with our nephew, Benjamin, and I certainly couldn't say no.

That's why after a long day **indoors**, I walked home, even though it was **pouring** outside. I really needed to stretch my **paws**.

I was just a few steps away from my front door when a blue **CAR** zoomed by at top **SPEED**. I was hit by a giant wave.

SPLAAASH!!!

Brrrrrr! The freezing water had soaked my **fur**.

Just then, I heard my cell phone. **BEEEP-BEEEP-BEEEP-BEEEP!**

I pulled the phone out of my pocket. On the screen was a picture of a water bottle labeled "**Icewater: Take a Dip in the Arctic!**"

I rolled my **EYES**. Clearly someone was pulling my tail. I wondered if it was my cousin Trap; he's the family **prankster**.

ALASKA

But it wasn't Trap. Instead, it was a **text message** from my dear friend Nicky. Her next message read: "Hi, Thea! We're in Barrow!"

The **THEA SISTERS** were five former students of

mine—*Colette*, *nicky*, PAMELA, PAULINA, and **Violet**. I met them while I was teaching a journalism course at their school, **MOUSEFORD ACADEMY**. We'd formed such a close bond that the five mouselets had named themselves after me!

Now, the name Barrow made my snout spin. Barrow . . . Barrow . . . I was sure I knew that name, but from where?

Aha! I had it at last. Barrow is the **northernmost** city in the United States! It's in Alaska! Moldy Brie, what was Nicky doing there?

The message continued: "I'm here with *Colette*, PAMELA, PAULINA, and **Violet**! Read the e-mail we sent you, and you'll get the full cheese!"

There was just one thing to do.

I **SCAMPERED** home, took a nice

I SCAMPERED home, took a nice long shower, and made myself a hot cup of tea.

long shower, and made myself a hot cup of tea. Then I curled up and got ready to read the newest adventure of my good friends the THEA SISTERS!

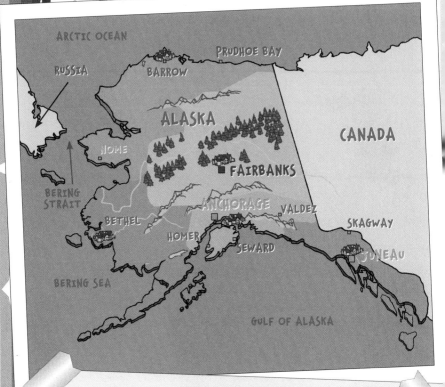

HISTORY

During the first half of the eighteenth century, Vitus Bering and Aleksey Chirikov explored the territory that became Alaska, and the famous captain James Cook visited it in 1778 during his hunt for the Northwest Passage to Europe.

Russia established a colony in Alaska in 1784 and for years profited from the land's natural wealth. But by the mid-nineteenth century, the Russian colonists had overhunted on land and sea, and the czar began to lose interest in the colony.

Russia sold Alaska to the United States in 1867. In 1912, it became an official territory of the United States. On January 3, 1959, it became the forty-ninth state.

ALASKA

Capital: Juneau

Largest city: Anchorage (more than 275,000 residents)

Surface area: 571,951 square miles. Alaska is the largest state in the United States.

Inhabitants per square mile: Ninety percent of the state has fewer than ten residents per square mile.

State motto: North to the Future

State nickname: Land of the Midnight Sun

GEOGRAPHY

Alaska is one of only two states in the United States that don't share a border with any other states (the other is Hawaii). In fact, Alaska's only border is with Canada. Most of the state is surrounded by the sea. The Bering Strait separates it from Russia.

BARROW

Barrow is the northernmost city in Alaska, and in the United States. During the summer, the sun is out for eighty-four straight days, even at midnight; in winter, the sun does not rise for the same period of time. Barrow's Inupiat name, Ukpeagvik, means "place to hunt snowy owls."

A VERY SPECIAL CONFERENCE

On **WHALE ISLAND**, home of **MOUSEFORD ACADEMY**, it was a brisk, chilly day. A **cold wind** was blowing from the north, a clear sign that winter was on its way. Even

the least bookish students were happy to stay inside the academy's **COZY** classrooms. On campus, mice scurried from one building to another as **quickly** as possible.

Paulina was in the computer lab, where she was reading an e-mail about the next Special Conference of the **Green Mice**[*], an environmental society she belonged to. It was an extraordinary occasion. The Special Conference took place every five years. During this **IMPORTANT** meeting, the Green Mice took a close look at the state of Earth's **HEALTH**.

Paulina glanced through the long list of participants and found her name and then her friend Nicky's name. They were just above another name that made her **heart** race like a rat in a maze: Ashvin Patna from the Green Mice in Delhi, India!

---

[*] Do you remember? The Green Mice helped the Thea Sisters in the book *Thea Stilton and the Secret City*.

Paulina had met Ashvin during a camping trip over the summer, and since then, she hadn't been able to forget his big black **EYES**.

Paulina was excited to see her friend again, and she was looking forward to the conference for another reason. The Green Mice had chosen to hold their meeting in remote Barrow, Alaska. Paulina had always wanted to travel to that region of the world.

"Barrow, **ALASKA**?!" Pamela exclaimed. She was shocked when Nicky and Paulina told their friends about their trip later that afternoon. "For the love of cheese! I'm so jealous, mouselets! I've always dreamed of zooming over the ice on a snowmobile!"

Colette, on the other paw, couldn't believe her friends were serious about this trip.

"The Arctic in **winter**? Has the **CHEESE** slipped off your cracker? Why would you expose your tender fur to such an **extreme** climate?"

Violet couldn't believe it, either, but for a different reason. "Is there really a branch of the **Green Mice** in such a remote part of the world?"

"There sure is!" Paulina confirmed. She added, "It's run by just one rodent, an **Inupiat** named Kanuk Krilaut. He is

INUIT

The Inupiat are the indigenous people of Barrow and much of northern Alaska. The word *Inupiat* means "real people." The Inupiat have been in northern Alaska for more than 4,000 years. Over the years, they have developed many ingenious ways to make use of the area's few natural resources.

The Inupiat are part of a larger, extended group of people known collectively as Inuit, or sometimes as Eskimo. The Inuit are also found in northern Canada, Greenland, and northern Asia.

president, secretary, and sole member of the club!"

"Well, it'll take you an awful long time to get **UP THERE**!" said Pamela.

"We'll be gone for at least a week," Nicky confirmed. "Maybe twelve days . . ."

That's when Violet realized something. "What about the competition? We almost forgot about the **competition**! We'll miss the deadline for the report if you spend twelve days in **ALASKA**!"

Violet was right: Paulina and Nicky had completely forgotten. . . .

PICTURES OF THE WORLD

Two weeks earlier, Professor Mousilda Marblemouse, the mouselets' **modern languages** teacher, had suggested they participate in a prestigious competition called Pictures of the World.

MOUSILDA MARBLEMOUSE

The contest was open to students, and winning a prize would be a real **honor** for the THEA SISTERS. So the mouselets had decided to present a report on **WHALE ISLAND**. Since then, they'd spent every spare moment writing and taking photos for their report.

Pamela was the first to squeak in defense of Nicky and Paulina's plans. "I think you should go to Barrow! There are zillions of competitions, but there's only one **SPECIAL CONFERENCE** every five years."

Nicky **SMILED** at her gratefully, but Paulina felt a little uncomfortable. She had made a promise to Violet, and she didn't want to **disappoint** her friend. On the other paw, her work with the **Green Mice** was very important to her. She didn't know what to do.

"You should try to convince them to hold the conference in a spot that's closer!"

Colette suggested. "And warmer! I hear the Hamster Islands are very nice this time of year. . . ."

"Let's call Ashvin and see if we can get the inside SCOOP," Nicky suggested.

Paulina agreed enthusiastically. She was already CONNECTED to the INTERNET. Quicker than you can say "pepperoni pizza with parmesan on top," she'd placed a videoconference call to India. Soon the screen lit up with the smile of the Indian mouseling.

HELLO, ALASKA!

"Hi, Paulina! I know why you're calling. You want to know why we've chosen a remote spot like Barrow, **ALASKA**, for our Special Conference, right?" ASHVIN said.

Paulina was surprised. "You took the words right out of my **MOUTH**!"

"At first, I wasn't so sure it was the right thing to do, either," Ashvin explained. "Then Kanuk presented us with an alarming report on the state of the glaciers."

The Thea Sisters crowded around the computer screen. Even Colette, Pamela, and Violet listened to Ashvin's explanation with interest.

"GLOBAL WARMING

has created some serious problems, especially for the glaciers and icebergs, which are melting. As if that weren't bad enough, Kanuk's **EQUIPMENT** has registered sudden changes to the sea ice. It's staying melted, as if it were **Summer** instead of the beginning of winter!"

The Thea Sisters exchanged looks. They were all thinking the same thing: They had to investigate what was going on in the **Arctic**!

The mouselets thanked Ashvin and said a quick good-bye. Once they'd logged off, there was a moment of silence.

Then **Violet** made a suggestion. "**Mouselets**, how about we *all* go to Barrow! We'll change the focus of our **report**. Instead of 'Pictures of Whale Island,' we'll call our report 'Pictures of Alaska'!"

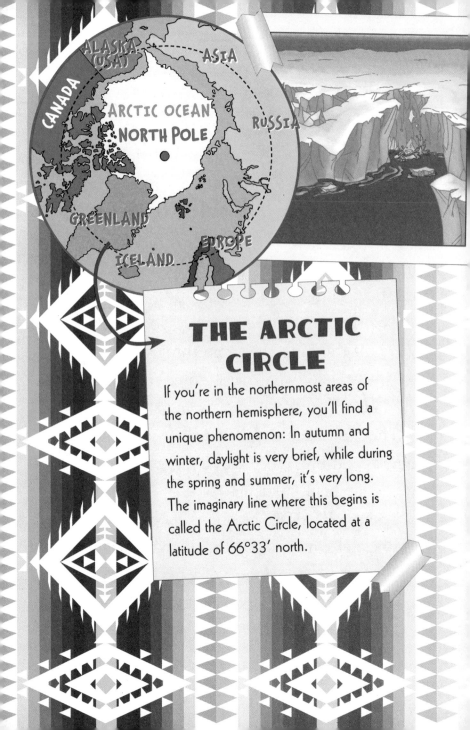

THE ARCTIC CIRCLE

If you're in the northernmost areas of the northern hemisphere, you'll find a unique phenomenon: In autumn and winter, daylight is very brief, while during the spring and summer, it's very long. The imaginary line where this begins is called the Arctic Circle, located at a latitude of 66°33' north.

SEA ICE

Sea ice is frozen salt water that forms and melts on the ocean. It can be found nearly everywhere in the polar regions, where very low temperatures cause the surface of seawater to freeze. Sea ice can blanket many square miles of territory. In the Arctic, it persists year after year, though some does usually melt in the summer and re-form in the winter.

GLACIERS AND ICEBERGS

Alaska is also home to many glaciers and icebergs. Unlike sea ice, glaciers and icebergs are made of freshwater or snow and usually form on land or lakes. Glaciers are land ice, while icebergs are chunks of glaciers that break off and float on the sea.

Since ice is less dense than water, icebergs float at the surface of the sea, though the part under the surface is much, much larger than what's above. Often only 1/6 or even 1/9 of the total size of an iceberg is visible above the water's surface. Because the wind, waves, and warmth from the sun erode the surface, icebergs get smaller and smaller until they disappear. The typical life span of an iceberg is three to six years. These enormous masses of ice — especially the parts below the surface — can easily damage the hulls of ships, so they pose a great danger to those who travel by water.

"**You said it, sister**!" Pamela shouted, slapping paws with Violet.

Everyone was **ENTHUSIASTIC** about the idea of going to Barrow. Even Colette was ready to risk freezing her delicate **fur** for such an important cause.

"I think it's a great idea! But what about getting permission?" Paulina asked, worried. "We're in the middle of the semester. Do you think *Professor de Mousus* will let us go?" Professor Octavius de Mousus was the headmaster of Mouseford Academy.

"Good point, Paulina," said Nicky, nodding. Let's go see the *Professor* right away."

Pamela was confident, as usual. "I just know he'll let us go! How could he let us pass up this **INCREDIBLE** chance to do some paws-on learning?"

A LONG WAIT

An hour later, the five MOUSELETS were huddled together outside the headmaster's office. They had been waiting in front of the closed door for quite a while.

Would *Professor de Mousus* agree to let them go to Alaska in the middle of the school

year? The **THEA SISTERS** weren't sure. So they had gone to *Professor Marblemouse* for advice.

"Pictures of Alaska? **Fabumouse!**" the professor exclaimed when she heard their idea.

Mousilda Marblemouse also had a great passion for the ENVIRONMENT, and she immediately understood how important it was for the mouselets to take this trip. In fact, she thought their report on Alaska might be the **PERFECT** opportunity to teach Mouseford Academy's students about issues affecting the polar regions.

So she had offered to squeak with the professor herself, to **describe** the mouselets' project and get the necessary permission.

But the minutes kept ticking by, and the

door to the headmaster's office stayed **CLOSED**, **SHUT**, **SEALED**!

Finally, Pam couldn't take it anymore. Even though she knew it was **rude**, she put her ear up against the door to listen.

"Pam! What do you think you're doing?!" Violet scolded.

"Shh! How can I be **quiet** as a mouse

when you're making all that **noise**?" Pamela shushed her.

At that moment, the door opened, and Pamela tumbled to the ground. The headmaster looked down at her in surprise.

"Uh, hi, Professor," she mumbled. "I just noticed, um, a loose hinge on your door over here, so I, um . . ."

Professor de Mousus smiled at her kindly. "Pamela, I don't need your help keeping my door on its hinges."

Pamela scrambled to her paws; her snout had turned bright RED with embarrassment.

"I can certainly understand why you mouselets are anxious," the professor continued. "I have some good news. You all may go!"

"Hooray!" the Thea Sisters exclaimed.

THE WAY TO ANCHORAGE

The **THEA SISTERS'** voyage was one of the longest and most **complicated** they had ever taken.

The next morning at **dawn**, they took the ferry to New Mouse City. Then they caught a **taxi** to the airport. After a very long flight, they reached **NEW YORK**. There, they had to switch to an **airplane** bound for Seattle, on the Pacific coast. In Seattle, they took yet another flight to Anchorage, **ALASKA**. Whew! What a trip!

Colette, who was seated by the window on the last flight, was the first to spot the SHIMMERING sea and the fjords along the coast.

"**LOOK!**" she cried.

Violet checked her guidebook. "We're flying over the Kenai Peninsula! Anchorage is located a little bit to the north, at the mouth of a bay called Cook Inlet. Actually, in just a few minutes, a long stretch of buildings and **SKYSCRAPERS** should appear, between the sea, the W☐☐☐☐, and the mountains. Then we'll know we've arrived in Anchorage."

Nicky was dazzled by the beauty and variety in the landscape. "Holey Swiss cheese, what an *incredible* place!"

"And it's such a modern city, even though it's right in the middle of the **BiGGeST** natural park in the world!" Pam added.

After they landed in Anchorage, the mouselets headed for the **Arctic Mouse Hostel**. That was where they were supposed to meet up with the other **Green Mice** before heading to Barrow.

As Colette, Nicky,

ANCHORAGE

Founded in 1914, Anchorage is the largest city in Alaska today, with a population of more than 275,000. Its economy is based on the extraction of oil and natural gas, and also on the fishing industry.

WELCOME,

Pamela, Paulina, and Violet scampered into the hostel lobby, they immediately spotted a large GREEN banner that read **Welcome, Green Mice**.

HISTORY OF ALASKA

The United States purchased Alaska from Russia in 1867 in a deal organized by Secretary of State William Seward. The amount paid was $7,200,000 (about two cents per acre). Despite this bargain, the purchase wasn't popular with most Americans, who considered Alaska a useless stretch of ice. The state was nicknamed "Seward's Folly" or "Seward's Icebox." Neither the Americans nor the Russians imagined that this "icebox" would become a source of petroleum, gas, coal, gold, and other precious metals.

FRIENDS FROM ALL OVER THE WORLD!

Nicky and Paulina were immediately surrounded by the Green Mice. All the members were **overjoyed** to see one another again. It was like a family reunion—of a big, friendly family with members from all over the world!

Nicky and Paulina introduced Colette, Pamela, and Violet. The group welcomed them with great enthusiasm. Outside, the temperature had fallen well below zero, but inside, the atmosphere was very **WARM**!

The mouselets went up to their room to wash up a bit, then came right down again for dinner. More than forty Green Mice were seated around a **long** table. They were cheerfully eating dinner: hot soup and

6 JOSHUA

8 CANDY

5 RONALDO

7 YUKO

sandwiches filled with **MELTiNG** cheese. But only a few of them were paying attention to their meal. They were all *busy* talking and listening and exchanging information about their journeys, their adventures, and the news from their corners of the globe.

Ashvin was always near the center of any lively conversation. He was more **POPULAR**

with the Green Mice than Santa Mouse! Nicky and Paulina immediately filled the seats next to him, while the other m**ice** in the club talked to him nonstop.

Colette began squeaking with a mouse to her right, who was very interested in hearing about living in *Paris*!

ALASKA'S WILDLIFE

The majority of Alaska is wilderness. There are moose and caribou, mountain goats, sheep, grizzly bears, polar bears, and wolves. Seals, whales, sea lions, puffins, and walruses live on the sea ice and in the ocean. In the summer, thousands of wild salmon leave the ocean and swim upstream to lay their eggs in freshwater. The sky is home to many kinds of birds, including the bald eagle, whose wingspan can be as long as eight feet!

BARROW AT LAST!

The next morning, the **Green Mice** hopped a flight bound for Barrow.

"Have you ever seen the Green Mice office in **BARROW**?" Nicky asked Ashvin, trying to start a conversation.

"No, not yet. It's only been around for a year, and so far it only has one member." He **SmiLED**. "But Kanuk is a true **FORCE** of nature! He's organized everything for the

BARROW

BARROW, Alaska, is located on the shores of the Arctic Ocean. It receives 24 hours of sunshine per day from mid-May to early August, while from mid-November to late January it is constantly dark: The sky is lit only by dim twilight, the moon, or the aurora borealis (northern lights).

conference. He's reserved his *parents'* entire hotel just for us!"

"A whole hotel just for us?" Colette asked.

"Well, I don't think it's very big," Ashvin replied. "And anyway, the tourist season in Barrow has been over for a while!"

The flight landed a short time later. As the Green Mice headed down the **staircase** to the tarmac, it was almost noon, and so outside, it appeared to be almost **NIGHT**.

The sunset shimmered on the horizon. Suddenly, as if the sky were welcoming them, a **fabumouse** aurora borealis appeared. Everyone stopped to gaze at it.

But they paused for only a moment. An icy wind had whipped up around them, and that hurried their pawsteps. *Sleet* stung their snouts with sharp **needles** of ice.

"*Brrr!*" exclaimed Paulina. "Let's move

AURORA BOREALIS

The aurora borealis is Earth's most amazing natural light show. It's caused by the interactions of protons and electrons in the atmosphere around the Earth's magnetic poles. These particles illuminate the air, giving the sky green, blue, and pink colors. For hours, the sky shines with these colored lights, which appear as iridescent arches and swoops. Galileo Galilei and Pierre Gassendi first used the term *aurora borealis* in the early seventeenth century.

those paws, **mouselets**! This place is chillier than Coldcreeps Peak!" She wrapped her coat around herself as tightly as she could.

Even Colette was glad that she had stuffed her beautiful hair under a big woolly beret. One thing was clear to everyone: The jackets and **boots** they were wearing wouldn't be able to handle this chill!

KANUK KRILAUT

"*Mukluks, asrgaaq,* and *parkas*! That's what you need to travel in Alaska!" This was the greeting they received from Kanuk, their host in Barrow. The young rodent pointed them in the direction of a shop inside the airport where they could buy clothes that were "North Pole–ready."

Never was a piece of **aDvice** more welcome!

"They're made in the traditional styles, but with **tECHNOLOGICaLLY** advanced materials. They're the best for protection against the **harsh weather** of the Arctic!" Kanuk explained.

"They're gorgeous!" Colette exclaimed, admiring the designs of the **aɾrgaaq**— that is, the gloves.

"And **SOFT**!" Pamela said, putting on a **parka** — that is, a padded jacket.

"And warm!" added Violet, who, thanks to some **mukluks**—that is, boots—could once more feel the blood moving in her frozen **paws**.

When everyone had chosen new clothes,

PARKA
(PADDED JACKET)

MUKLUK
(BOOT)

ASRGAAQ
(GLOVE)

Kanuk exclaimed, "Great! Now you're ready for the deep freeze. Okay, so here's your next challenge—choose whether you'd like to ride in an all-terrain vehicle or on a **snowmobile**."

At the word snowmobile, Pamela leaped to her paws and sped out of the store *faster* than the mouse who ran up the clock. As soon as she reached the parking lot, she JUMPED into the driver's seat of the biggest snowmobile.

"Kanuk, you have to let me drive this thing! PLEASE, PLEASE, **PLEASE!**"

Kanuk took one look at her and burst out laughing. "Pamela, that snowmobile looks just perfect for you!"

HOTEL KRILAUT

Kanuk's **family's** hotel was located in a neighborhood that was more deserted than a cheese shop the day after Christmas. The group of **friends** quickly crossed the empty gray **STREETS**. The houses all

looked the same. They were low to the ground and very plain in design.

In spite of the WARM clothing they'd bought, the Green Mice were shivering in the stiff, icy wind. Even the mice from colder climates weren't used to temperatures as low as these!

The only one having fun was Pamela. She pushed her snowmobile as hard

as it could go, and she whooped and cheered every time it bumped over a snowdrift.

Kanuk signaled as they drew close to the hotel. If he hadn't, none of them would have been able to tell the difference between it and the cabins around it.

Kanuk noticed his friends' confused expressions. "Were you expecting a deluxe SKYSCRAPER?" He smiled. "All the buildings in Barrow are low because the ground is completely frozen! We have to build on wood pilings on the ground, so the cabins can't WEIGH too much or the wood will crack."

PERMAFROST

In very cold places, the soil is frozen even deep down. For this reason, it is called permafrost—that is, the soil is permanently frozen. However, the top layer of ice does melt partially when the temperature rises. This is why homes must be built on wooden pilings, which are driven into the deeper and more solid layers of ice.

As he squeaked, he opened the door of the hotel, and a **rainbow** of color greeted the new arrivals!

The outside of the hotel might have been cold and gray, but the inside was cozier than a fake cat-fur blanket. **Fluffy** carpets and gorgeous multicolored rugs covered

the floor. The walls had beautiful wood paneling, and the living room was filled with soft sofas and lots of paintings.

"Beautiful!" Nicky exclaimed, walking up to the largest **painting** in the room. "Who's the artist?"

"My grandfather," Kanuk replied. "He's a painter, and my little brother, Pamik, is following in his **pawsteps**. The hotel is full of their work!"

Kanuk's family met the new arrivals with big welcoming *smiles* and pots of hot **tea**.

INUPIAT PARTY!

The **THEA SISTERS** and the Green Mice spent their first afternoon having fun and getting to know each other. Kanuk was truly a wonderful host. With the help of his younger brother, Pamik, he organized a **party** in the courtyard in front of the hotel.

Everyone wanted to participate.

Nicky and Pamela sang with the Screaming Icicles, a rock goup made up of really cool rodents! Everyone **enjoyed** it except Violet, who preferred classical music.

Paulina participated in a **wild** curling match. She was on the same **team** as Ashvin and Kanuk.

CURLING

Curling is a team sport that is played on ice. There are four players on each team, and they take turns trying to slide smooth, heavy granite stones across the ice onto a circular target.

Pamela was one of the first to line up for a snowmobile race. She finished **second**, right behind Pamik.

Halfway into the festivities, Kanuk's grandfather joined them, dragging a large, **HEAVY** blanket behind him. He asked the **strongest** mouselets and mouselings to join him.

"Hold on tight to the edges," he told them. "This is a *mapquq*, which means 'trampoline-blanket.' Once, we **Inupiat** used it to jump high in the air so that we could **LOOK** far into the distance, across the icy regions, where there were neither trees nor hills to block our view!"

The Thea Sisters looked at one another in 𝔰𝔲𝔯𝔭𝔯𝔦𝔰𝔢.

Grandfather continued, "Today we still use it the same way, but for different reasons.

It's great for exercise and for doing somersaults in the AIR!"

"**Ooh! Ooh!**" Nicky and Pamela immediately put their paws in the air. They couldn't wait to *JUMP UP* on the *mapquq*.

"Whee! Whee!" they cheered as they spun around in midair.

Colette shouted in **time** with the others. Ashvin grinned at her and grabbed her paw. "Come on! Let's try it next!"

Colette was a little AFRAID, but she couldn't say no. Soon she was leaping higher than a flying squirrel!

Paulina and Nicky **noticed** Colette with Ashvin, and each mouselet felt a *flash* of jealousy. But they quickly brushed it off. After all, Colette was one of their best friends!

WHAT HAPPENED TO ERNANEK?

The **party** was still going stronger than New Mouse City's annual CheeseFest, but Kanuk was growing **restless**. While the others were having fun, he kept glancing over at the horizon.

Violet noticed and went over to squeak with him. "What's wrong, Kanuk? Is bad weather coming?"

He replied, "No, it's not that. It's just that he isn't here yet. And he promised!"

"Who are you talking about?" Violet asked.

But Kanuk's **grandfather** interrupted. "Kanuk, you know that Ernanek can't stand the city! How could you think that he would come here, into the middle of a crowd?

He's a **solitary** rodent. He prefers to live by himself, with only his DOGS for company. He's always **out** on his sled, and when he decides to rest, he builds an IGLOO!"

"But he *promised* me!" Kanuk said **stubbornly**. Then he turned to Violet and explained, "Ernanek is a dear friend of my grandfather's. I'm very attached to him. He knows so much about this area that I asked him to come **squeak** to the Green Mice about the changes that are happening in the **Arctic**. And Ernanek *always* keeps his promises!"

Now even Kanuk's grandfather was

IGLOO

An igloo is a shelter made out of blocks of snow, generally in the shape of a dome. Although the word *igloo* means "house" in the Inuktitut language, a true cabin made of snow is referred to by the more precise name *igluvigak*.

watching the horizon with concern. The sky was almost completely **D A R K** : The last light of dusk was fading.

"If that's true, then I'm sure he'll be here soon!" Kanuk's grandfather said.

As darkness fell, the temperature became **unbearable**.

"Time to go inside, mouselets," said Pamela, shivering. "I'm **freezing** like a mousicle out here!"

The Thea Sisters and the Green Mice scurried into the hotel. They were still full of **CHEER** from the party, and they couldn't stop *laughing* and **JOKING** around. Until . . .

"**SILENCE!**" Kanuk thundered.

The Green Mice were caught by surprise. Immediately, everyone was silent.

"LISTEN . . . ," Kanuk added, lowering his squeak to a WHiSPeR. He put his ear up against the window.

It was so quiet you could have heard a cheese slice drop. But no one heard a thing — except for Kanuk. He ran to the door and threw it open. He had heard the far-off barking of a dog on the wind.

AWHOOOOOOOOO!

ALASKAN MALAMUTE

The Alaskan malamute is the oldest and biggest of the Arctic sled dogs. It is a sturdy animal with strong muscles. Used to extreme situations and hard work, it's a loyal and devoted animal, born with a strong instinct and great intuition. The malamute is named after the Inuit tribe the *Mahlemut,* who settled in Alaska hundreds of years ago.

Kanuk scampered out into the icy darkness of the Arctic night.

"KIMMIK!"

"WOOF! WOOF! WOOF!" came the reply. A big dog bounded up to greet him.

Kimmik was a gorgeous sled dog, an Alaskan malamute with wolf **blood**. Kanuk explained that he was Ernanek's lead sled dog.

But how had he gotten here all **alone**?

Kanuk took the dog by the collar and

brought him into the **WARMTH** of the hotel. The poor animal looked exhausted.

Kanuk motioned to his friends not to come too close, to avoid **SCARING** Kimmik. He moved the dog onto a rug and gave him something to eat and drink while he rubbed his body with a woolen blanket. He **DRIED** the dog, warmed him, and reassured him all at once.

"Kimmik, where is Ernanek?" Kanuk asked at last. "Where did you leave the sled and the other dogs?"

Kimmik turned his nose toward the front door and **LET OUT** a long howl.

AWHOOOOOOOOO!

What could have happened to Ernanek? Why had his dog come to Barrow alone?

kimmik, LEAD
SLED DOG

"Ernanek must be in **DANGER**!" Grandpa Krilaut squeaked. "Sending us his lead sled dog is a cry for help!"

"You're right, Grandpa," Kanuk said. "I'm going to go look for him. There's no time to lose!"

"But it's twenty degrees below zero out there!" observed Joshua, who wasn't used to the cold yet. Even inside the hotel, he was wearing his parka. Just thinking about going out sent a shiver down his tail.

"That's why I need to GO and find him immediately!" Kanuk declared.

"I'll go with you!" Ashvin said. "In the DARK, four eyes can see better than two!"

"Count us in, too!" PAMELA said,

squeaking for all the **THEA SiSTERS**. They had no intention of waiting around in the hotel for news.

Only Colette was a little **reluctant**. "**Achoo!** Mouselets, I don't think I can go along this time. . . . **Achoo! Achoo!** I think I'm coming down with a cold. . . ."

"Don't worry, Colette," Violet said, comforting her. "It's better for you to stay

WHAT A FUNNY LITTLE SNEEZE!

ACHOO! ACHOO! ACHOO!

SHE ALWAYS SNEEZES LIKE THAT.

warm. This weather could chill you to the **tailbone**!"

"Do you have any idea where we should start looking?" asked Annika, the kind mouse from the Netherlands.

"Kimmik will guide us," Kanuk replied. "See? He's already **RECOVERED** and eager to return to Ernanek!"

It was true! After he'd finished eating, the dog had **JUMPED UP**. He was scratching his paws against the door, eager to go out.

Kanuk harnessed his own pack of dogs to the sled but let Kimmik go free so that he could run ahead and guide them through the **NIGHT**.

Ashvin and Pamela jumped onto two snowmobiles. Nicky and Paulina both wanted to **Sit** behind Ashvin, but there was room for only one, and Nicky got there first.

Paulina found a place behind Pam, but she couldn't help shooting her friend a dirty **LOOK**.

Violet quickly climbed onto Kanuk's sled and settled under a warm blanket. But she had noticed her friends' silent **argument**, and she'd felt the **tension** in the air ever since they'd met Ashvin at Anchorage. Their **jealous** looks worried her. Could two of the THEA SiSTERS be feuding over **Ashvin**?

THE PACK

"Pack" is the name given to a group of dogs that pulls a sled. The leader of the pack is the dog that dominates the others. It is stronger, more intelligent, and more skilled, so it becomes the lead dog.

The person who drives the sled is called the musher. The musher gives vocal commands in various tones of voice. The word *mush* comes from the French word *marchons* (which means "let's go"), an order that was often used in the French colonies in Canada.

AN EXPLOSION
IN THE NIGHT

The little group headed out into the night. It was **darker** than the inside of a cat's belly. Soon they had **DISAPPEARED** from the view of the party that had stayed behind at the hotel. For a while, Colette and the others could still hear the barking of the dogs and the **ROAR** of the snowmobiles' motors.

WOOF WOOF WOOF WOOF WOOF WOOF!!!

VROOOOOOOMMMMMMMMMMMMM.

Outside, Kimmik led the way at a steady *FAST* pace. He was impatient to find Ernanek. That dog was a true champion! The pack of dogs pulling Kanuk's sled sped along with great energy.

But the true contest was between the two **snowmobiles**: Ashvin was going at full throttle, and Pamela wanted to go just as fast. If he **JUMPED** straight over a ditch, she made her snowmobile fly over the next one.

Nicky held on tightly to Ashvin, but not because she wanted to be close to him. She was **TERRIFIED** of being thrown off!

Paulina assumed that Nicky was doing this out of *affection*, and encouraged Pam to keep up with them.

"Let's stay together! Don't lose sight of them!" she cried. But what she really wanted to say was "I don't want Nicky to be alone with Ashvin!"

If only she had known what was going through her **FRIEND'S** head! You see, Nicky wasn't so sure she wanted to be sitting on

Ashvin's snowmobile anymore!

The motor's roar was DEAFENING, but Nicky thought she heard Ashvin exclaim, "WOW! These sure are powerful snowmobiles!"

Could he actually be having fun at a time like this?! When they were racing through the frigid Arctic to rescue a rodent in trouble?

Nicky couldn't believe her ears. Suddenly, Ashvin didn't seem quite so charming.

Her thoughts were interrupted by an earsplitting noise.

BOOOOOMMM!

CLUE!

The icy ground shook. Nicky practically LEAPED out of her fur.

Pamela was so scared she almost lost control of the snowmobile. Even the dogs had stopped running.

"Frozen fish sticks, what just happened?" Paulina CRIED.

Kanuk noticed cracks in the ice and looked worried. "An explosion!"

An explosion in the middle of the Arctic night? What could have caused it?

A LONG DISCUSSION

Meanwhile, back at the hotel, the **Green Mice** were looking for ways to pass the time while they waited.

"ACHOO! ACHOO!"

Colette couldn't stop sneezing, so Pamik brought her a cup filled with a warm, **smelly** brew. It was made from fish oil and dried herbs from the tundra.

"This is a real miracle cure! My mother always makes it for me when I have a **cold**. By tomorrow, you'll feel much better!" Pamik assured her.

Colette took one sniff. **PEE-YOO!** It was stinkier than the stinkiest blue cheese! She wrinkled her nose. "Thank you! But I'm already feeling better. **ACHOO!**"

Pamik gave her a skeptical look. "Try it. You'll see. It'll help you!"

Colette realized that Pamik was going to insist. So she held her nose and drank the **brew** in one big gulp. Then she opened her **eyes** wide and covered her snout with her paw. In all her life, she'd never tasted anything so **disgusting**! It was all she could do not to toss her cheese.

BLEEEAH!

"Colette, you're **paler** than a slice of mozzarella!" Annika said, looking at her with **concern**. "Do you feel all right?"

Colette coughed a few times. "Well, after that delicious concoction, I'm sure I'll feel much better!"

Everyone around her started to **laugh**. They began chatting about this and that:

food, **MOVIES**, **computers**, **sports**....

Then Yuko started talking about Ashvin. Like Nicky and Paulina, she had a little crush on him. "Ashvin is a real **CHAMPION**! He's good at practically any sport!"

"Oh, really?" replied Eric, looking **envious**. "Champion of what? I'm sure he's never participated in a real cross-country skiing **MARATHON**, like I have."

Ronaldo, the mouseling from Mexico, quickly interrupted. "I'm a champion at **JUMPING** on a trampoline, that's for sure!"

"And I've climbed the **HIGHEST** peaks in the Alps!" Giovanni, the Italian, added, not wanting to be left out.

"And I've swum across the English Channel!"

"And I have a **BLACK BELT** in karate!"

"And I go skydiving!"

Everyone had something to boast about.

Eventually Pamik, who had been listening closely, exclaimed, "I went fishing on a real **UMIAK** this summer!"

Everyone turned to look at him.

"What's an umiak?" Colette asked. She had never heard the word before.

Pamik pointed to a painting on the wall, which showed a group of rodents fishing at **SEA** amid floating ice. "It's our traditional boat. My **grandpa** still has his umiak from when he was a young mouseling! Would you like to see it?"

A STORY FROM THE PAST

Grandpa Krilaut shook his snout, doubtful. He cared greatly about his umiak and treated it as if it were a valuable **antique** to be admired. He didn't want to share it with a bunch of young rodents who had no interest in Inupiat traditions.

"Come on, Grandpa, everyone wants to see it," Pamik cajoled him.

"It's true!" said Annika. "Will you show us?"

Grandpa Krilaut took one look at the **curious** and **ENTHUSIASTIC** expressions of the young mice and changed his mind.

GRANDPA KRILAUT

"First I must explain a few things to you," he said. "With your eyes, you see only an **old** boat. But you must also look with your **heart**. Only then can you understand what the **UMIAK** means to the Inupiat people."

Grandpa Krilaut took out an old photo **album** and started to flip through it. "This is the **LAND** of the Inupiat. A land

WE HAD TO USE ICE TO BUILD OUR HOUSES.

WE HAD TO MAKE EVERYTHING BY PAW.
EVERYONE HAD TO CONTRIBUTE.

of **ICE**: no fields to plant, no trees for the **WOOD** needed to build houses or boats . . . or even to build a **FIRE**!"

He paused and then continued. "You arrived here by **plane**, but when I was young, there was *only one* ship that came here each summer. It was the only way to get here. Everything that the ship carried was expensive and very *precious*, because there was no other way to get things! Then the ship would leave and we wouldn't see it again for a whole year."

The young mice listened breathlessly. Colette couldn't imagine how they could survive in a world without **fruit**, without **flowers**, without shops and clothes and **makeup**!

Grandpa continued. "There weren't any **snowmobiles** or motorboats back then. We had to do everything with our paws. We used whatever **materials** were at our disposal! And so, for centuries and centuries, my people lived this way, hunting and fishing."

Grandpa pointed to the large painting on the wall. "To face the **sea**, we needed boats. But we didn't have a lot of **WOOD** to

TO FACE THE SEA, WE NEEDED BOATS, SO WE INVENTED THE UMIAK!

build them! That's why we invented the UMIAK!"

Grandpa got up and motioned for the young mice to follow him. He led them to a shed connected to the hotel by a **long** corridor.

Inside, in the center of the room, was the wooden SKELETON of a small boat, covered in leather sewn to its frame.

"Here it is!" the old Inupiat said, running his paw along the keel affectionately.

Ivan gave it the once-over. "That's it?! But if I climbed on top of it, it would definitely TIP OVER!"

"HA! HA! HA!" Grandpa Krilaut laughed heartily. "Is that what you think, sonny rat?! And yet this UMIAK can hold eight mice! I've fished from it all my life."

Eric scampered around the boat, admiring it from every angle. "It's so LIGHT. . . . It must really speed through the water!"

"It goes SUPERFAST!" Pamik confirmed. "But steering it isn't so easy. It requires a lot of SKILL!"

A CRY IN THE NIGHT

At the same time, out in the icy darkness, Kanuk cracked his whip in the air. "**YOP! YOP! YOP!**" he cried. The pack was falling behind, losing sight of Kimmik.

Right after the **mysterious** explosion, Ernanek's lead dog had leaped ahead, barking. But the cause of the **EXPLOSION** was still unknown.

By now they had reached Nanavak Bay, a wild area **SOUTHWEST** of the city of Barrow. It was barren and completely deserted.

Kanuk wasn't sure exactly where Kimmik had gone. He couldn't distinguish his faraway bark from the nearby, **earsplitting** barking of the pack. Kanuk loosened his grip on the reins to let his lead dog follow

Kimmik: The dog's senses of smell and hearing were much **BETTER** than his.

Ashvin had stopped *GUNNING* his snowmobile. He was sticking closer to Kanuk than a glue trap. The last thing he

wanted was to lose sight of his friend out in the frigid Arctic night.

The **darkness** of the night around them was so thick that Nicky's ♡HEART started to beat faster. She lost her breath, something that usually happened to her only in small, narrow places. (Nicky suffered from claustrophobia.) But this place, and the pitch **DARKNESS**, made her feel panicky.

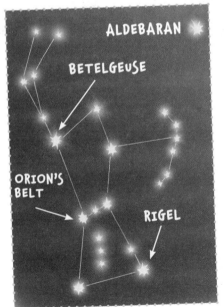

ALDEBARAN

BETELGEUSE

ORION'S BELT

RIGEL

Relax! she told herself. *You're out in the open, not closed in!* She looked around, but the total darkness seemed to press in on her.

Then she raised

her **EYES** to the sky, and with great relief she saw the STARS. How beautiful!

She recognized Aldebaran and Orion's Belt. According to mythology, Aldebaran represented a snorting bull, and the stars that made up the constellation Orion represented the hunter **battling** it.

THE STARS

On the icy expanse of the Arctic, knowledge of the sky is essential to knowing one's location. This knowledge was handed down from generation to generation. When men went to find food, they were joined by their entire families. During the journey, the father would explain the positions of the stars to his sons, and while they rested, the mother would tell the children stories about the sky.

Finally, her breathing returned to normal. Thinking about the stars helped Nicky distract herself from her **FEARS**.

Suddenly, a shout broke the silence. "**Help!**"

It was Pamela! The headlight on her **snowmobile** was pointed straight ahead . . . at a pack of **ferocious** wolves who'd just leaped out from behind a snowdrift!

Pamela *swerved* to the side at the last minute. The sudden movement made the **snowmobile** fly through the air like a **GERBIL** falling off his wheel!

Pamela and Paulina were hurled from their seats. A moment later, they landed in the **snow**.

A SHELTER IN THE SNOW

Luckily, it wasn't wolves that had frightened Pamela, but Ernanek's dog pack! Ernanek himself was perched on the highest mound of **SNOW**. He was cradling a dog in his paws as if it were a baby mouseling. They were **SAFE**, although they were both **HURT**.

Ernanek had **dug** a shelter in the snow — a temporary place where he and his dogs could wait for help to arrive. He was sure that Kimmik would go alert someone. Ernanek knew his

ERNANEK

loyal lead dog wouldn't **ABANDON** him!

Kanuk ran to Ernanek. "Come on. Grab on to me. We'll take the injured dog on my sled!"

Ernanek leaned on his shoulder, looking at him *gratefully*. "My dear mouseling, I knew that you would come to rescue me!" he said in Inuktitut.

Violet helped him get comfortable on the sled, right next to Kanuk.

"What about Ernanek's dogs?" Paulina asked, alarmed. "We're not leaving them here all alone, are we?"

"Don't worry, they'll **FOLLOW** us!" Kanuk assured her. "That is, they'll follow Kimmik."

When they reached the hotel, Grandpa Krilaut scampered out to meet them. As soon as he reached Ernanek, he *hugged* his old friend with relief.

Violet couldn't understand a word the two old Inuit said to each other, but their faces were beaming. They were happier than two mice in a pantry filled with CHEESE as they greeted each other affectionately.

Kanuk's grandfather fed Ernanek and his dogs and gave Ernanek warm clothing. Once they were all warm again, Ernanek started to tell everyone what he had seen out on the ice. . . .

ERNANEK'S STORY

Although Ernanek was tired and pale, his **EYES** blazed with the intensity of those of a cat on a mouse hunt. He spoke in the Inuktitut language, which Kanuk **HURRIED** to translate.

"I was traveling to Barrow, where I had been invited by my **friends** the Krilauts. I was looking forward to squeaking with the Green Mice about the ecological changes I've observed over my lifetime. I was near Nanavak Bay when I heard an explosion."

Pamela's eyes widened. "Just like the one we heard!" she exclaimed.

Ernanek nodded.

"That's right, Ernanek, we heard an explosion, too!" Kanuk agreed.

Ernanek continued, with the help of Kanuk's translation. "So I went to **SEE** what had caused the noise."

The young mice held their BREATH.

"There was a huge ship. It looked like an icebreaker. The words *Seagull* and *Vancouver* were written on its stern."

Ernanek spoke softly, using short sentences, to give Kanuk time to translate. "There were a few rodents on the sea ice. I

CLUE!

wanted to go ask them what was going on. But as soon as they saw me, they started to **yell**! I didn't understand what they said, but they were definitely HOSTILE!"

"They threatened you?!" asked Paulina, concerned.

Ernanek guessed the meaning of Paulina's words. "I heard them yelling and knew I needed to get back to the sled *quickly*. Then . . . another boom! The earth trembled, and the **sled** flipped over. A huge wall of ice SHATTERED right behind me!

"Do you understand? They were using explosives!" The old rodent put his paws over his snout, as though he had just

A mysterious ship with an unfriendly crew, and more explosions. What's going on in the Arctic?!

BOOOMMMM!

WOOF WOOF WOOF

remembered something very PAINFUL. "Splinters of ice were flying everywhere! One of them hit me, and others hurt my dogs!"

The THEA SISTERS were shaking. They were madder than a rat with its tail

caught in a trap. So were the rest of the **Green Mice**.

"I couldn't go on; my dogs were too hurt!" Ernanek continued. "So I sent my loyal **friend** Kimmik to you for help."

The dog **CURLED** up at Ernanek's feet, as if he had understood what Ernanek had said.

FIRST, SOME RESEARCH

"I say we teach those rascals a lesson!" exclaimed Ashvin, who had been silent up to this point.

"Yes, we must stop them!" Kanuk said. "I don't know what they're up to, but using dynamite could cause serious **damage** to the ECOSYSTEM!"

The THEA SISTERS agreed, but they weren't sure what they should do.

"Of course we have to STOP them!" Violet chimed in. "But let's not forget that this could be DANGEROUS."

"Violet's right!" Paulina said. "Before we do anything else, we've got to find out a bit more about who these mice are."

"We have the name of their ship: the

Seagull from **VANCOUVER**!" said Nicky. "Maybe we can find out more on the Internet."

"Wise words!" **Grandpa Krilaut** said approvingly. "Paulina, why don't you see what you can find out? For the rest of us, the best thing to do is get some rest. It's the

middle of the night, and you mouselets have made a **long** journey. Ernanek needs to regain his **STRENGTH**! We'll meet in the morning and decide on a course of action."

The **young** mice obeyed. They all went to their rooms, squeaking nervously.

The THEA SISTERS were sharing a room. Paulina immediately pulled out her laptop and started doing some research on the **Internet**.

Because of her COLD, Colette was having a hard time falling asleep. She joined Paulina at the computer. Soon all five mouselets were gathered around the glowing screen.

"I don't understand why they would **BLOW UP** the ice," Nicky said thoughtfully. She was stretching her paws on the floor, which was what she always did when she was nervous.

"Maybe they're looking for something," Violet guessed.

"Here it is!" Paulina cried when she found the name *Seagull* on a website.

Crunch. "Did you find out who the rats from the ship are?" *Crunch*. Pamela spoke while nibbling on a cheese cracker. (When Pam was anxious, she always munched on something crunchy.)

"Not yet," Paulina replied. "But now that I have some basic information about the ship and its owner, I can put out a query to my friends around the WORLD. By the time we wake up tomorrow, we'll have more information. Now, come on, mouselets. Let's get some sleep. . . ."

A HAPPY SURPRISE!

A pleasant surprise greeted Colette the next morning: Her nose was completely clear!  Could Pamik's stinky **brew** have already had an effect on her? It looked like the answer was **YES**!

Feeling cheerful, she headed for the window and threw it open so that she could admire the view.

WHOOOSH! An icy WiND forced her to close it immediately.

"Brrr! It's colder out there than iced cheese!"

Then she looked outside again, confused. "But . . . what time is it? Why is the sun already **setting**?"

Violet rubbed her eyes and **giggled**. "Colette, it's eight o'clock in the morning. The sun doesn't stay up long in the fall!"

"**Chewy cheese croissants!**" Colette exclaimed, smacking her snout. "I forgot

we're in the **ARCTIC CIRCLE**!"

All the squeaking had woken Paulina. She immediately turned on her **laptop**. But she was **DISAPPOINTED**: She had received a number of e-mails from friends, but there wasn't any news about the ship.

"No news about the *Seagull*. We'll have to wait a bit longer," she sighed.

"Well then, why don't we get some Breakfast?" asked Pam. "I'm hungry as a wolf!"

The rest of the THEA SISTERS agreed. They scurried down to the dining room and found the other Green Mice already having breakfast. Mama Krilaut had prepared a delicious meal: tea, milk, and hot **chocolate**; berry jam; "fabumouse muffins" (so named by PAMELA); and bannock, a flat oat bread, hot off the stove! Mama Krilaut had made it by paw, according to an old family recipe.

Colette, Nicky, Pamela, Paulina, and Violet were so focused on this yummy breakfast that they didn't notice that there were a few mouselings missing from the meal.

After her second helping of bannock, Nicky looked around. "Is everyone else still sleeping?" she asked Annika.

Surprised, Annika replied, "What? Didn't you know? They left last night!"

Paulina's milk **went down** the wrong way. "**Cough! Cough! Cough!** Wait, what do you mean, **they left**?!"

"For where?" Pamela asked.

"For **Nanavak Bay**! They just couldn't wait, I guess."

"Kanuk went?" Nicky asked in disbelief.

"Yes, and Pamik, too," said Annika. "Ashvin convinced them they had to go right away."

Candy, the mouse from South Africa, and Yuko, the JAPANESE mouse, joined the conversation.

"We saw them last **NIGHT**. They took the snowmobiles, the all-terrain vehicles—everything!" Candy said, looking DISAPPOINTED. "So now we can't leave the hotel unless we go on paw!"

Pamela was **annoyed**. "Ashvin could have warned us! I thought we agreed this was going to be a group decision."

Yuko defended Ashvin. "I'm sure Ashvin just wanted to help. He's so **IMPULSIVE**.

He can't stand injustice, and he always wants to help the helpless!"

"We can't **STAND** injustice, either!" Pam shot back. "But in this case, we said we'd all act *together*! We're supposed to be a team!"

"Okay, let's stop ARGUING amongst ourselves," Paulina said. "Right now, the most important thing is that we're stuck here! We've got to focus on finding a way to leave the hotel so we can **JOIN** the others."

mineRAL WATER!

Disappointed, the mouselets returned to their rooms. None of them could believe that the others had left **the night before**.

"It's not fair! Going off like that and keeping it **SECRET** from us!" Pamela fumed.

"I can't believe Ashvin did that!" Nicky said. "And to think I thought he was cute!" She *glanced* at Paulina.

"Well, he *is* cute!" Paulina said with a **smile**. "But it looks like he might not be the brightest rodent in the bunch!"

Violet agreed. "Exactly! It never occurred to him that we should form a plan together before heading out into the **freezing** tundra. It was really thoughtless."

Paulina looked at Nicky, **embarrassed**. "I was jealous of you because of him."

"And I was jealous of you!" Nicky said.

They burst out laughing. **"HA! HA! HA!"**

"Let's make a vow, mouselings," said Colette. "We'll never let a crush come between us again!"

All the mouselets nodded in relief.

"What is it Thea always says?" Violet tried to remember.

"Friends together! Mice forever!" cheered Nicky.

"FRIENDS TOGETHER! MiCE FOREVER!"

CHORUSED the mouselets.

But then they remembered what was going on.

"Cheese niblets,

I hope they don't get into any trouble out there!" Violet said. "Going snout-to-snout with HOSTILE rodents, without any background or any kind of plan . . . This could turn into a real cat-astrophe!"

Violet's words cast a CHILL over the other mouselets.

Paulina checked her **laptop** to see if any news about the *Seagull* had come in. This time, she wasn't disappointed. "'The *Seagull* is the old icebreaker *Botnia*, which was renamed when it was sold,'" she read out loud. "It belongs to a business called *Icewater*, owned by **Malcolm Ratt**. And listen to this: His factory bottles mineral water!"

"**Mineral water?!**" Nicky and Pamela cried together.

Violet's eyes opened wide. "That means

those rodents are using **dynamite** on the icebergs . . ."

"So they can turn them into mineral water!" Paulina finished her sentence.

"But how can they make a **profit**?!" Pamela asked. "A bottle of mineral water hardly costs a dollar."

"It's much more than a dollar!" Colette answered. "*Icewater* is served in the most famouse and exclusive **restaurants** in the world! It costs more than twenty

MINERAL WATER

Mineral water is water that contains dissolved minerals. These minerals are believed to have health benefits. Water can be described as "mineral water" if it comes from an underground layer or pool and bubbles up through a natural spring.

Mineral waters are divided into different categories based on the presence or lack (and the percentage) of specific minerals.

dollars a bottle. I've heard some rodents even use water from icebergs to wash their fur. They say it makes your fur shinier!"

"That's crazier than a cat chasing his own tail," said Violet, shaking her snout.

WHAT SHOULD THE THEA SISTERS DO?

1) Ernanek discovered an icebreaker whose crew was using dynamite to break up icebergs. When the rodents saw him, they threatened him!
2) The icebreaker belongs to Icewater, a business that sells mineral water.
3) The Thea Sisters believe that Icewater is using Alaska's iceberg water to produce the most famouse (and expensive) water in the world. Do you think they're right?

A DISTRESS CALL

If the **THEA SISTERS** were worried, Grandpa Krilaut and Ernanek were close to panic. The boys had **SLIPPED AWAY** in the night. Even Pamik had gone with them!

Outside, the wind had started to blow even more fiercely than it had the day before.

WHOOOOOOSSSSSH!

The Thea Sisters rejoined the **mouselets** and Grandpa Krilaut and Ernanek in the living room.

"What should we do?" Grandpa Krilaut asked the group. "If we wait too long, those mouselings will end up **FROZEN** like fish sticks!"

"I think we have some information that

could help," Pamela announced. "We know who the ship belongs to. Does the name **Malcolm Ratt** mean anything to you?"

Grandpa Krilaut had heard it before. "He was a **fur** merchant years ago," he said with a look of disgust. "But he hasn't been seen in these parts for a long time."

"Now he bottles mineral **water**," Paulina explained. "Apparently the water from **icebergs** is very fashionable with **VIRs***!"

"Are you saying that he's destroying the icebergs just to make bottled water?!" Annika exclaimed. "If that's true, we need to alert the **POLICE**! At the very least, those scoundrels have injured Ernanek!"

Grandpa Krilaut agreed. "That's right. But it will take a long time for them to get here from Anchorage. If something

* VIR = Very Important Rodent

happens to our **mouselings** in the meantime, I'll never forgive myself!"

There was a pause for a moment while everyone tried to think of what to do next. All of a sudden, **FOUR** cell phones went off at the same moment!

BEE-BEE-BEE-BEEP BEE-BEE-BEE-BEEP BEE-BEE-BEE-BEEP BEE-BEE-BEEP!

Annika, Nicky, Paulina, and Candy hurried to **read** the messages they had just received.

It turned out to be the same message sent to the four friends. Kanuk had sent it **SECRETLY** and in a hurry: WE'RE PRISONERS!

Annika was the first to react. "I'm calling the police right now!"

"Yes, right away!" Nicky agreed. "But we can't just stay here and wait. The ship could leave with the mouselings on board. . . . Every minute is PRECIOUS!"

"But how can we get to them? On paw?!" Candy asked. "They've left us here without any **vehicles**, and we don't have sleds!"

The THEA SISTERS looked at one another.

"Did they take Ernanek's sled?" Paulina asked.

"No," Grandpa replied. "But it's not very **big**. It can hold three rodents at most, and that includes the driver."

"The UMIAK!" Colette whispered.

Pamela didn't understand. "What did you say?"

"The umiak! The umiak!"

Grandpa Krilaut shouted. "With the boat, we might get there *faster* than on a sled!" Then he stopped, glancing at his old friend. "But Ernanek and I can't do it alone."

Nicky had already decided. "I know how

to steer a boat! And my friends can certainly **MANEUVER** an oar!"

Pamela **winked** at Colette. "Of course! Even Colette will risk ruining her manicure for a good cause, right?"

Colette stuck out her tongue playfully at her friend.

"So it's decided!" Paulina concluded. "We'll go with you. Together we'll find the icebreaker!"

GREASY ICE AND PANCAKES

When Grandpa Krilaut turned on the light in the shed, Violet, Nicky, Paulina, and Pamela were struck **squeakless**.

This was Grandpa Krilaut's boat?! He couldn't be talking about that dusty old thing resting on wooden sawhorses . . . could he?

At the sight of the old boat, Colette's idea lost some of its BRILLIANCE. The umiak didn't look very impressive.

Ernanek limped into the shed last. He circled the boat inch by inch. The old Inupiat's eyes shone with excitement. For him, the UMIAK was as precious as jewelry.

"I wouldn't trust that boat to make it through the ice — not for all the cheese in the world!" Paulina whispered to Nicky.

"It does seem awfully light, but if the Inupiat have used them for centuries, they must work!" Nicky replied. "And it's the only way we can save our friends!"

"Okay, the boat's ready!" Colette said BRISKLY. "But how do we get it in the water if the sea is frozen?"

"It's not completely **FROZEN**!" **Grandpa Krilaut** said. "That's exactly the problem Kanuk brought you here to discuss: **global warming**. It's making the sea ice in the Arctic melt for much of the year! And this is damaging the environment. But today this problem will work in our favor. It'll make it much easier to reach the *Seagull*."

Grandpa Krilaut and Ernanek started gathering the equipment they'd need. "When I was a young mouseling, the ship routes were all closed due to ice at this time of year," he explained to the **mouselets**. "Now, because of the higher **temperatures**, the ice melts into thin, round sheets, which we call 'grease and pancakes.' And we can **ROW** through this 'greasy' ice!"

"Grease and pancakes? Did I hear that right?!" Violet asked the other mouselets.

"The sea doesn't freeze quickly," Ernanek explained. "First it forms thin plates of ice, which FLOAT and give the surface an oily look. That's why it's called GREASY ice. Then the plates start to bump into each other. They take on a **circular** shape, with raised edges. They end up looking like big pancakes!"

Grandpa Krilaut and Ernanek placed the umiak on two WOODEN boards, as if they were skis. Then they fastened it to the sled and invited the THEA SISTERS to get in.

The little group was ready to go!

ROWING ON THE ICE

The **THEA SISTERS** were **excited** to make the **voyage** on the umiak. But once they lowered the little boat into the **waves**, it seemed more fragile than ever.

Grandpa Krilaut helped the mouselets take their seats and gave each her own oar. "The most important thing is to row all together. I'll set the rhythm, and you must try to follow it."

The sky was even **DARKER** than it had been the day before, with black storm clouds as far as the eye could see. The sea was rougher than a cat's tongue.

"I know it sounds crazy, but this weather is good news for us," Grandpa Krilaut observed. "If the sea is moving, it won't **freeze**."

The mouselets could see with their own eyes what Grandpa had meant by "grease and pancakes."

"**YUM!**" said Pam, pretending to lick her whiskers. She pointed at the wide patches of **ice**. "They really do look like pancakes. Chewy cheesecake, it's a good thing we ate such a big breakfast or I'd be hungry right about now. **HA! HA!**"

"It's so **DARK!**" Nicky observed. "We should have brought **flashlights**."

"No, it's better this way," said Violet. "Those slimy **sewer rats** won't be able to see us coming. Our only advantage is the **ELEMENT OF SURPRISE!**"

"You're right," Grandpa agreed. "Do you feel how the current is **PUSHING**? It's moving us in the right direction!"

Grandpa Krilaut started to row. He soon set the rhythm.

"OOO-YOP! OOO-YOP!"

The **mouselets** worked hard. They didn't have much experience on the sea, but they were determined to rescue their friends.

After they'd rowed for a while, they didn't feel the **COLD** anymore. Colette noticed that she was practically **sweating** beneath her parka.

"Keep the **rhythm**," Paulina reminded her. She was sitting right behind Colette. "Otherwise, we'll crash into each other!"

Colette rowed a bit too **VIGOROUSLY**, and the handle of her oar knocked against Nicky's back.

"**OWWW!**" Nicky yelped.

"**STOP!**" Grandpa Krilaut ordered. "This isn't working! Your **strength** isn't balanced."

He pointed his paw first at Colette, Paulina, and Violet. "You, you, and you: Use more of the strength in your arms!"

Then he turned to Nicky and Pamela. "You need to hold back a little bit of your **energy**! There are five of you — try to work together like five fingers on a single **paw**!"

The Thea Sisters followed his suggestion, and the boat began to speed up, smooth as **CREAM CHEESE** on a bagel.

THE ICEBREAKER

Nicky's eyes had adjusted to the **dark**. She was the first to catch **SIGHT** of Nanavak Bay. "Look!" she cried, pointing. The **icebreaker** was still there, anchored a short distance from the mouth of the bay.

Grandpa Krilaut signaled to the **mouselets** to stop rowing. Only he and Ernanek

continued steering the boat, which slipped through the waves as silently as a cat stalking a mouse.

As the UMIAK drew closer to the ship, they could hear the muffled sounds of machinery from within. Some of the portholes were lit up. They didn't see anyone on the sea ice, nor was there any MOVEMENT on the deck.

"We've got to get up there so we can figure out where the other mouselings are being held prisoner," Nicky whispered.

"I don't see any guards," Violet observed. "And look—there's a ladder!"

Pamela stamped her paws. "Great! Let's start CLIMBING. What are we waiting for?"

But Paulina wanted to make sure they had a solid plan. "Hmm, why don't we go up and check out the **captain's** cabin first? Then we can spread out below deck. That's where the other cabins are. If it's all clear, we can meet up and check out the hold together."

"I'm coming too!" **Grandpa Krilaut** said. "Since Ernanek is injured, he'll stay behind and look after the UMIAK."

COUNT ME OUT, OKAY?

A few moments later, the **THEA SISTERS** were peeking through the window of the captain's cabin. They spotted nine rodents arguing **heatedly**. It seemed like they were trying to make an important decision.

"With these mouselings underpaw, we can hardly work!" the captain said **ANGRILY**. He had just hung up the phone after a long call with the owner of *Icewater*. "Now we have to head for port with the hold half empty!"

"Half empty?!" protested a SKiNNY rodent with red fur. He looked like an old **SEA** rat. "Half empty means half pay, and that adds up to a big problem for me!"

"Let's wait another day and set off all the **DYNAMITE**!" replied a rodent with a tattoo of a cobra on one arm. "All we need is one good **boom!** and we can fill the ship with ice treasure. Then we'll work on it during the **VOYAGE.**"

"I don't like this, Cobra," grumbled a rat as big as a boxing champ. "I don't like it at all, okay?"

Cobra didn't like being **questioned**. "What don't you like about my plan? It's **PERFECT**!"

"I work for **Mr. Ratt**, owner of *Icewater*, okay?" the big mouse responded. "I'll do everything that's needed to get the job done. But I'm not keeping those mouselings **PRISONER**!"

The **captain** intervened. "They were snooping around! And then we found out they're members of Green Mice. We all know that **BLOWING UP** the **icebergs** is illegal. Once these meddling mice turn in Mr. Ratt, they'll have us arrested, too! It's too **risky**!"

The whole crew agreed with him — everyone except the **BIG** mouse, who continued shaking his head. "I don't like it. I don't like it at all, **OKAY**? When we

started, all we had to do was work. Now there's this horrible business with these **mouselings** we've taken as prisoners. I don't want to do anything **WRONG**, okay? I don't like it, and **you can count me out**!"

TROUBLE ON BOARD

The argument in the **captain's** cabin raged on. And that was a lucky break for the THEA SISTERS! The CRIMINALS were so busy squabbling among themselves they didn't even notice that the **mouselets** and Grandpa Krilaut had slipped on board!

"Let's make the most of this messy situation," Nicky whispered. "We've got to go find the mouselings and release them!"

The other mouselets **nodded** in agreement. But they still didn't know where their friends were being held, so they had to **scurry** and find them quickly.

The mouselets and **Grandpa Krilaut** scattered along the hallway that led to the cabins, trying to open the doors.

Nothing. All the doors were locked, and no sounds were coming from inside.

Just then . . . **THUMP!** A noise **StaRtLeD** Colette. There was someone behind the door closest to her.

Just then, her nose started to itch, and . . . **"ACHOO! ACHOO!"**

Her sneezes burst out one after another, and there was nothing she could do to stop them!

"*Colette?*" came a squeak from behind the door.

Grandpa Krilaut recognized that squeak right away.

"Pamik!"

They had found the mouselings! Now it was time to free them. The Thea Sisters needed to get the keys, but they certainly couldn't **FACE** nine sailors alone.

Back in the captain's cabin, the argument had grown even more **INTENSE**, and the big mouse had been overpowered. The others wanted to **L°CK** him up with the mouselings.

"We've gotta get this **TATTLETAIL** under lock and key!" the captain said. "Go get the keys so we can shut him up in one of the cabins!" he ordered Flea, the puniest of the group.

Flea nodded and headed for the closet.

It was just the opportunity **Grandpa Krilaut** and the **THEA SISTERS** had been waiting for!

Flea had just **GRABBED** a bunch of keys when he heard a deep, menacing squeak behind him. "Give me those keys, or I'll put your tail in one heck of a twist!"

Flea shivered and turned around slowly: Grandpa Krilaut and the mouselets were standing there, their most **THREATENING** looks on their snouts. Caught by **surprise**, the little rodent was unable to resist them.

While Grandpa Krilaut locked Flea into one of the other cabins, the five Thea Sisters **Ran** to release the mouselings.

Now the moment had arrived for them to go snout-to-snout with the slimy sewer rats aboard the *Seagull*!

A TWIST!

Meanwhile, in the captain's cabin, the captain was starting to **WONDER** what had happened to Flea. He was just calling for him when someone appeared at the door.

"Not so fast, **Cheesebrain**!" declared Pamela. "We've found our friends and we've released them!"

Pamela, Nicky, Kanuk, Ashvin, Pamik, and three other **Green Mice** stood in the doorway, blocking it.

There was a moment of stunned silence.

The big mouse took advantage of the moment to **liberate himself** from the rodents who had him pinned. With one **POWERFUL** shake, he was free. The scoundrels who'd been holding him

crashed to the ground, and the mouselets and mouselings trapped them.

Only the large mouse remained on his paws.

WHAT NOW?

The Thea Sisters and the Green Mice weren't sure what to do. This **ENORMOUSE** mouse was twice as tall as they were!

Pamela took control of the situation. "Your FRIENDS are **MEANER** than a pack of

hungry cats, aren't they?" she asked the big mouse. She had a feeling that he was good at heart, and that he might prove to be a **valuable** ally.

The big mouse seemed confused: He had never had **BAD** intentions. He wanted to explain that he didn't have anything to do with the capture of the **mouselings**. But he was nervous, and he couldn't seem to come up with the right words.

At last, he found his squeak and said, "I work hard and I don't want to hurt anyone, okay?"

"**Right on, pal!**" said Pamela. "It's obvious that as a mouse, you're *okay!*"

WOP-WOP-WOP-WOP-WOP-WOP-WOP!

Suddenly, they heard the sound of a helicopter.

The **POLICE** had arrived!

An Apology

The police found eight **rats** wrapped up like presents on Christmas morning. One big rodent was holding them down.

"These CRIMINALS destroyed entire icebergs with dynamite just to make mineral water!" Ashvin exclaimed.

While the policemen were busy taking the scoundrels into their custody, Paulina told Ashvin, "We already knew about the mineral water. And we've also informed the authorities that the **MASTERMIND** behind all this is one **Malcolm Ratt**, owner of Icewater. I found all this information by doing research on the **INTERNET**!"

"Oh!" Ashvin exclaimed, BLUSHING. "Mouselets, I owe you an apology. I really had my **whiskers** tangled on this one. You gathered more information with your computer than we did with our **RECKLESS** nighttime mission. I was so eager to do something, I ended up dragging the other mouselings into this **mess**!"

Colette, Nicky, Pamela, Paulina, and Violet looked at one another. A moment earlier, they had wanted to give Ashvin an earful. But now?

Pam turned to Ashvin. "You know what, Ashvin? You're a half-cooked pizza and all your **PISTONS** are jammed. But on the other paw, I have to give you a pat on the tail for owning up to your **MISTAKES**!"

Ashvin's mouth fell open in confusion. "Wh-what did she just squeak?" he **stuttered**, turning to Nicky and Paulina.

Nicky and Paulina just laughed. "Pamela

is one saucy mouselet! HA! HA!! HA!!!"

Ashvin led the police and the **THEA SISTERS** to the ship's hold. Before they had been captured, the mouselings had discovered the *Seagull's* secret.

The hold had been **transformed** into an ice factory: Blocks of pure **ice**

were **CRUSHED** (as if to make a giant snow cone) and melted. The **water** was then bottled and packaged up in **CRATES**, ready to be shipped.

When the ship reached its **PORT**, the cargo would be ready: **THOUSANDS** of bottles would be sent to the most **fashionable** restaurants in the world!

TiME TO CELEBRATE!

The next day, all the rodents in Barrow dressed up for a **party** in honor of the Green Mice, the **THEA SiSTERS**, **Grandpa Krilaut**, and **ERNANEK**!

Reporters had broken the story of the **scoundrels'** arrest. **Malcolm Ratt** had been captured at the Seattle airport,

where he had been about to **_make a run for it_**.

The party was a hit, with lots of merry singing and dancing and whisker-licking-good traditional Inupiat food.

The **THEA SISTERS** mingled with the crowd and sang at the **TOP OF THEIR LUNGS** with the Screaming Icicles. Afterward, they sat down with Kanuk and Pamik and stuffed themselves with more of Mama Krilaut's yummy bannock!

As for Ashvin, Nicky and Paulina had forgiven him, but he no longer held any special *charm* for them. So they were **happy** to see him walking paw in paw with Yuko.

Throughout the day of the party, the **icy** town of Barrow was transformed into the happiest, warmest, and most **colorful** spot on the planet! And **magically**, as if just for this special occasion, a gorgeous **aurora borealis** appeared in the sky, leaving everyone squeakless.

Nicky, Pamela, Violet, Paulina, and Colette hugged one another tightly. They were **DELIGHTED** to have concluded another adventure together. Even the sky seemed to be reminding them that no **treasure** was more **precious** than friendship!

PICTURES OF ALASKA

It was late at **NIGHT** by the time I had finished reading my FRiENDS' story. After their adventure, the Green Mice held their Special Conference as planned. Ernanek stayed in Barrow and squeaked about all the climate changes he had witnessed over the course of his **long** life. His interview was broadcast by the local television station and was sent to news programs all over the world. The **Green Mice** were hoping against hope that by raising awareness, they might be able to slow down the problems of **global warming**.

While Nicky and Paulina participated in the conference, *Colette*, PAMELA, and **Violet** focused on finishing their report.

Rather than limiting themselves to Barrow and its surroundings, they rented a small airplane to visit all the most beautiful places in Alaska.

In fact, along with their e-mail, I found an attachment that contained the first draft of their report, "Pictures of Alaska, an Icy Treasure." They asked me for some **editorial** advice on how to

improve their report, and for an opinion on their work.

What is there to say? Their report was fascinating, a real **page-turner**. The THEA SISTERS had done it again!

Thea Sisters

Want to read the next adventure
of the Thea Sisters?
I can't wait to tell you all about it!

THEA STILTON AND THE
SECRET OF THE OLD CASTLE

When the Thea Sisters' good friend Bridget has to return to Scotland to help her family repair their ancient castle, the five mice offer to help Bridget however they can. And when their friend goes missing, the Thea Sisters have to rush to Scotland to help find her! Along the way, the five friends encounter Celtic legends, cryptic messages, and hidden treasures on a trip that's full of mysteries and surprises!

And don't miss any of my other fabumouse adventures!

THEA STILTON
AND THE
DRAGON'S CODE

THEA STILTON
AND THE
MOUNTAIN OF FIRE

THEA STILTON
AND THE GHOST OF
THE SHIPWRECK

THEA STILTON
AND THE
SECRET CITY

THEA STILTON
AND THE MYSTERY
IN PARIS

THEA STILTON
AND THE CHERRY
BLOSSOM ADVENTURE

THEA STILTON
AND THE STAR
CASTAWAYS

THEA STILTON:
BIG TROUBLE IN THE
BIG APPLE

Be sure to read these stories, too!

#1 Lost Treasure of the Emerald Eye

#2 The Curse of the Cheese Pyramid

#3 Cat and Mouse in a Haunted House

#4 I'm Too Fond of My Fur!

#5 Four Mice Deep in the Jungle

#6 Paws Off, Cheddarface!

#7 Red Pizzas for a Blue Count

#8 Attack of the Bandit Cats

#9 A Fabumouse Vacation for Geronimo

#10 All Because of a Cup of Coffee

#11 It's Halloween, You 'Fraidy Mouse!

#12 Merry Christmas, Geronimo!

#13 The Phantom of the Subway

#14 The Temple of the Ruby of Fire

#15 The Mona Mousa Code

#16 A Cheese-Colored Camper

#17 Watch Your Whiskers, Stilton!

#18 Shipwreck on the Pirate Islands

#19 My Name Is Stilton, Geronimo Stilton

#20 Surf's Up, Geronimo!

#21 The Wild, Wild West

#22 The Secret of Cacklefur Castle

A Christmas Tale

#23 Valentine's Day Disaster

#24 Field Trip to Niagara Falls

#25 The Search for Sunken Treasure

#26 The Mummy with No Name

#27 The Christmas Toy Factory

#28 Wedding Crasher

#29 Down and Out Down Under

#30 The Mouse Island Marathon

#31 The Mysterious Cheese Thief

Christmas Catastrophe

#32 Valley of the Giant Skeletons

#33 Geronimo and the Gold Medal Mystery

#34 Geronimo Stilton, Secret Agent

#35 A Very Merry Christmas

#36 Geronimo's Valentine

#37 The Race Across America

#38 A Fabumouse School Adventure

#39 Singing Sensation

#40 The Karate Mouse

#41 Mighty Mount Kilimanjaro

#42 The Peculiar Pumpkin Thief

#43 I'm Not a Supermouse!

#44 The Giant Diamond Robbery

#45 Save the White Whale!

#46 The Haunted Castle

#47 Run for the Hills, Geronimo!

#48 The Mystery in Venice

And coming soon!

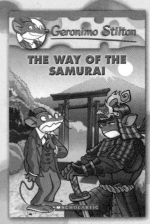

#49 The Way of the Samurai

Don't miss these very special editions!

THE KINGDOM OF FANTASY

THE QUEST FOR PARADISE:
THE RETURN TO THE KINGDOM OF FANTASY

THE AMAZING VOYAGE:
THE THIRD ADVENTURE IN THE KINGDOM OF FANTASY

Meet
CREEPELLA VON CACKLEFUR

I, *Geronimo Stilton*, have a lot of mouse friends, but none as **spooky** as my friend CREEPELLA VON CACKLEFUR! She is an enchanting and MYSTERIOUS mouse with a pet bat named Bitewing. YIKES! I'm a real 'fraidy mouse, but even I think CREEPELLA and her family are AWFULLY fascinating. I can't wait for you to read all about CREEPELLA in these a-mouse-ly funny and **spectacularly spooky** tales!

#1 THE THIRTEEN GHOSTS

#2 MEET ME IN HORRORWOOD

THANKS FOR READING,
AND GOOD-BYE UNTIL OUR
NEXT ADVENTURE!

Thea Sisters